It's Bedtime TITCH

Pat Hutchins

A Red Fox Book

Published by Random House Children's Books
20 Vauxhall Bridge Road, London SW1V 2SA

A division of Random House UK Ltd
London Melbourne Sydney Auckland
Johannesburg and agencies throughout the world

A Hutchins Film Company Limited production for Yorkshire Television

1 3 5 7 9 10 8 6 4 2

First published by Red Fox 1998

Printed and bound in Hong Kong.

RANDOM HOUSE UK Limited Reg. No. 954009

ISBN 0 09 926648 2

It was Titch's bedtime.
Mum had read him his
favourite story, *Little Red
Riding Hood.*

'Time to go to sleep,' said Mum.

'Where's Tailcat?' Titch asked, 'He always comes to see me before I go to sleep.'

'He must be in the garden,' said Mum. 'He doesn't like the noise from the football match on television, and neither do I.

'I'm going over to Auntie Margaret's until the game has finished. Good night, Titch,' Mum said, turning out the big light.

Titch tried to sleep.
   But he thought he heard his cupboard door open.
He sat up to look - and it had opened!

Of course he knew it wasn't a wolf, but he went downstairs to tell Dad anyway.

'Dad, Dad!' said Titch, 'I think there's something in my cupboard!'

'Titch!' cried Peter and Mary and Dad. 'Move! We can't see the game!'

'But my cupboard door opened,' said Titch. 'Come and see!'

'You take Titch upstairs, Mary,' said Dad. 'I don't want to miss the goal kick!'

Mary didn't want to miss the goal kick either, but she took Titch upstairs.

Mary looked in the cupboard.
'Look!' she said. 'There isn't
anything in the cupboard.
Now go to sleep!'

Titch tried to sleep.

But he thought he heard a noise under the bed.

Of course he knew it wasn't a wolf, but he went downstairs to tell Dad anyway.

'Dad, Dad! There's a noise under my bed!'
  'Move, Titch!' cried Peter, Mary and Dad. 'We can't see the game!'

'But there's a noise under my bed,' said Titch. 'Come and listen!'

'You take Titch upstairs, Peter,' said Dad. 'I don't want to miss this bit!'

Peter didn't want to miss that bit either, but he took Titch upstairs.

Peter put the light on.

  'There isn't anything under the bed,' said Peter.
'Look! Now go to bed!'

Titch tried to sleep with the light on.

But he thought he saw the rug move.

He was *sure* he saw the rug move.

Of course he knew it wasn't a wolf, but he went downstairs to tell Dad anyway.

'Dad! Dad! My rug moved!'

'Not now, Titch!' cried Peter, Mary and Dad. 'This is the most exciting part!'

'But my rug moved!' said Titch. 'Come and see!'

'All right Titch,' said Dad. 'I'll take you up this time. And I want you to go straight to sleep!'

'See,' said Dad. 'The rug isn't moving. Now into bed with you. Good night!'

Titch really tried to sleep.
   But what was that? And that? And that?!

Titch had to go downstairs and tell them that there *was* something in the cupboard, *and* under the bed, *and* under the rug.

And of course it wasn't a wolf...

...it was Tailcat!